THE DRAGON AND THE MOUSE

"TOGETHER AGAIN"

written by

DR. STEPHEN A. TIMM

illustrated by

LALO

Library of Congress Cataloging in Publication Data
Timm, Stephen A.
THE DRAGON AND THE MOUSE: TOGETHER AGAIN
SUMMARY: A dragon and a mouse are friends, but
miscommunication, jumping to conclusions and
unnecessary worry cause a near disaster.
[1. Fairy Tales. 2. Dragons — Fiction] I. Title.

ISBN 0-939-72804-4

Published by Touchstone Enterprises, Inc.
Fargo, North Dakota

Printed in the United States of America.
Library of Congress Catalog Card Number: 81-90230

WITH LOVE TO MY PARENTS
AND MY CHILDREN, WHO
HAVE BEEN AND ARE, MY TEACHERS.

In some other land, a dragon and a mouse were the best of friends. One day, the dragon flew to visit the mouse.

When he arrived, the mouse was gone. The dragon thought, "Gee, I wish the mouse were here. I'll leave a note for him."

DRINK
POP
SODA
WELCOME

He never used paper and pencil. Instead, he found a huge stone nearby. He lugged the rock to the house.

On the rock he blasted a message with his fiery breath. The message said, "Don't go away, I'll be back soon." Then he flew away.

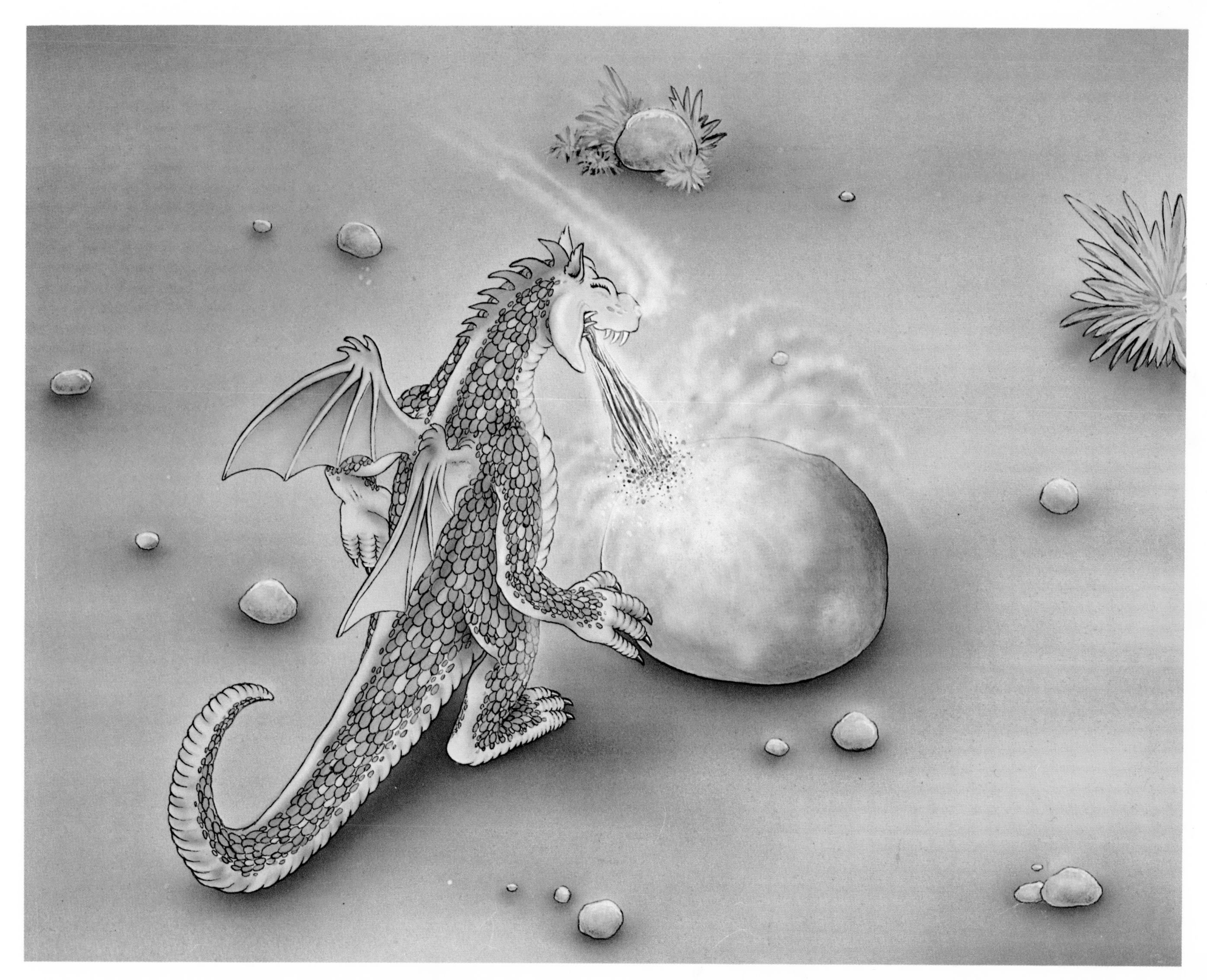

Later, the mouse came home. He saw dragon footprints all around. When he saw the great big rock, he discovered the message.

He looked and looked, but could not read the words on the rock. All he could see were scribbles. The mouse thought the message said, "I'm going far away, maybe to the moon."

When the mouse read this, he became heartsick. He imagined the dragon flying to the moon. Would he be eaten by a moon creature? Would he be lost in space forever? The mouse thought such terrible thoughts, he shook with worry.

After a while, the mouse thought, "I'm going to the dragon's cave! Maybe I can stop him!" He quickly packed some clothes and took a little bit of food. He was in such a hurry, he left everything a mess.

Then, he set out. How sad and lonely he felt. The mouse kept thinking, "Will I ever see my friend again?"

He walked, and walked, and walked.

At last, he came to the cave. He tiptoed inside. The cave was cold and dark. No dragon.

He sat down. He shivered with cold. Then, he began to cry.

Later, the dragon returned to his friend's house. He peeked inside. He saw something terrible! Dresser drawers were open! The bed was not made! Clothes were lying on the floor! Alarmed, he thought, "What has happened? The mouse always keeps his house neat and clean! He's been robbed! Maybe kidnapped too!"

POP

The dragon said to himself, "I will search for him and find him no matter what!" He puffed himself up and became even more fierce. Then, he flew off to save his friend.

Meanwhile, the mouse kept sitting in the cold, dark cave. He sat and he sat and he sat. "Oh, what has happened to my friend?" he thought.

Suddenly, the cave rumbled and shook! "Oh, no! Something terrible is happening!" thought the mouse. He jumped from his chair to find a place to hide. Then . . . CRASH! A huge foot slammed down on the floor of the cave. The mouse was almost crushed! He spun around to see! There stood . . .!

. . . the DRAGON!

The mouse was so surprised and happy, he hugged the dragon's leg. The dragon, when he saw the mouse, almost shouted with joy, but thought, "I don't want the mouse to know I was worried."

So, instead, he gently picked up the mouse and whispered, "Hello, little one. Why are you here?" The mouse squeaked, (he was so excited, all he could do was squeak), "I thought you had flown to the moon! I thought you were lost in space!"

The dragon frowned, set the mouse down, and said, “Why that’s silly. You shouldn’t be such a worrier.”

Then he bent down and said kindly, "Why don't you stay here tonight? I'll start a fire so we can warm ourselves." The mouse thought for a while and said, "Gladly, I will."

The dragon started a warm fire in the huge fireplace. Then, they sat by the fire and talked late into the night, both happy to be together again.

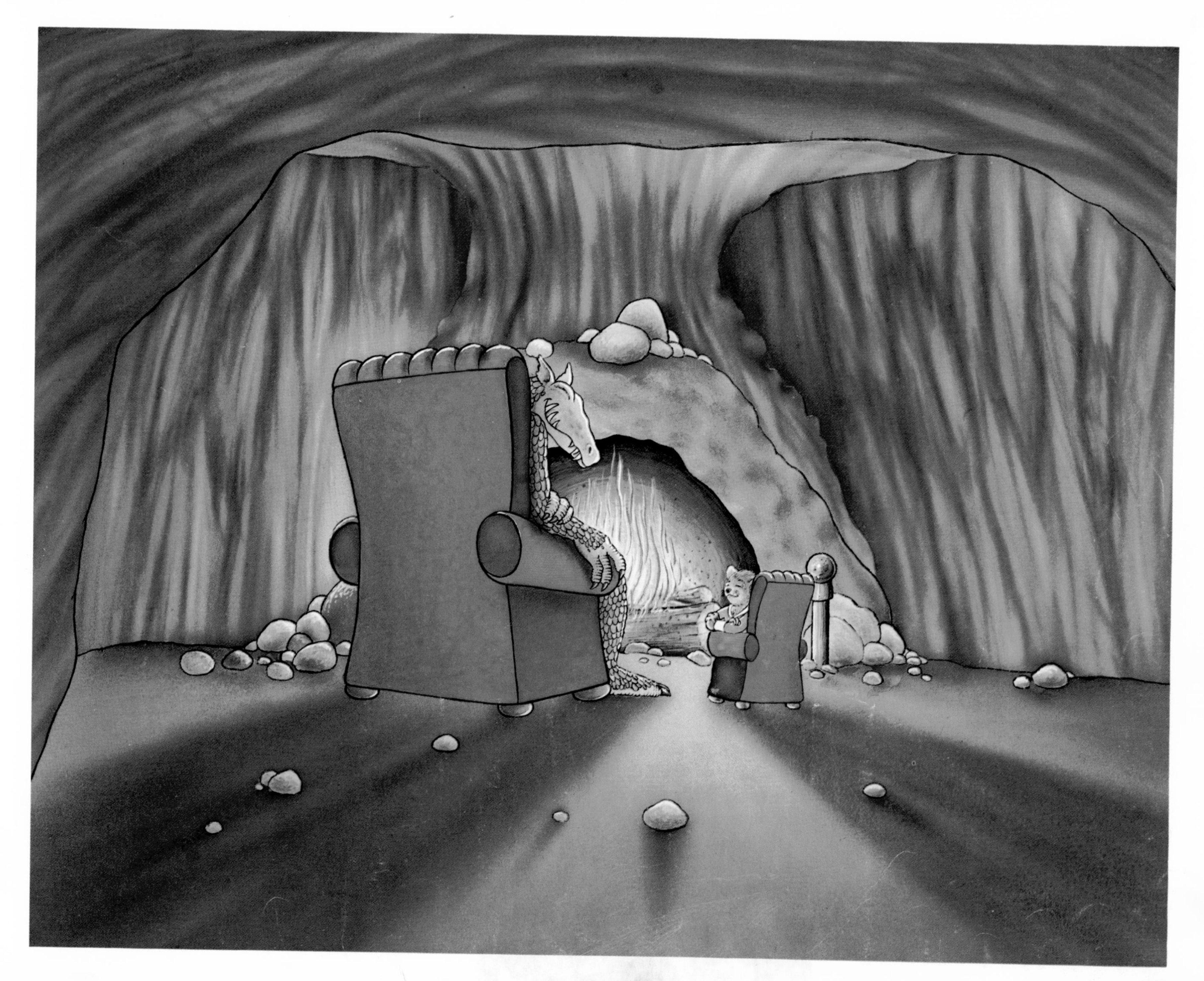

About the author:

Dr. Stephen A. Timm was born in Fairmont, Minnesota, where he lived until age 14, when he moved to Fargo, North Dakota. He received his bachelor's degree from Westmar College, Le Mars, Iowa, and his doctorate in clinical psychology from the University of Nebraska at Lincoln, Nebraska. Currently, he is in full-time private practice in Fargo where he resides with his wife, Marcia, and their three children. He has written another book titled, **The Dragon and the Mouse**. As an educator, lecturer, human resource consultant, and psychotherapist, he works extensively with children and adults, assisting them with the challenge of living successfully and abun[illegible]ntly.

Abou[illegible]e artist:

Wh[illegible]t can be said about the [illegible] these times when life is a high-[illegible]d chase where people [illegible] through time, LALO is in the d[illegible]'s seat. With all exits [illegible]shes through with ma[illegible]nt speed and unacce[illegible] [illegible]y and then emerges tri[illegible]tly without a SCRA[illegible]

[illegible] a person of many dif[illegible] [illegible]d abilities. He prefers the [illegible] maginator." Lalo b[illegible] [illegible]e must never forget tha[illegible]e i[illegible]tion with [illegible] is like having wings with [illegible]"